TO FACE A LION

G.D.K. Huffman

gdkhuffman.com

Library of Congress Control Number: 2023923716

ISBN 978-1-963222-03-6 (paperback)

ISBN 978-1-963222-02-9 (ebook)

To all the people who supported me even when I chose a harder path.

And to my God who pushed me to follow it.

To Face a Lion

"You should have known this would happen," he broke the silence as they both looked toward the grove in front of them, the last of the underbrush being stamped into the ground as he spoke. Nothing but dust and blood would fill that space. "Lresech is close to you, but she's also a very good warrior, or did you think you were the only one to notice?"

From beside him on the log, Ieltsech shot his friend a glare to hide his intense discomfort with the situation. "I have known Sech my whole life Tiech, I think I know why I'm here," after saying this though, his eyes returned to the ground between his feet. He had been there a long time, as evidenced by the ash-cold fire pit and the various words drawn into the dust at his feet. In fact he was drawing yet another symbol in the dirt with the butt of his hefty axe, whether a prayer or frustration his friend could not tell.

"I am aware," Tiech replied, shaking his head and beginning to find his own shoes rather interesting as well. "That's why I thought you might have been a little more prepared for this. But I suppose it could sneak up on any of us." Silence between the two followed as they observed their sturdy deerskin boots, but thankfully it was filled by the noise of the clan around them.

While they were sick to their stomach, the rest of the two tribes were ecstatic with what was about to happen here. Even though it would only be one fight, the victor would earn the right to challenge the legendary Lresech, counted among the greatest warriors of the Bounding Deer clan. Even though she wasn't a chief, none had expected there would only be two fighting to earn that right. But the reason for this was quite obvious when Stetes was taken into account, and even his challenger was having serious doubts as to whether his move had been wise or not.

Across the way stood the giant, his green muscles glinting in the sunlight as he talked to his friends around him, almost as if mocking the two on the opposite side. Already decked out for battle, the mighty Stetes did not need to think which word he wanted painted on his face and shield. He had fought enough battles to know which words would lead him to success: 'glory' was already written in red upon his forehead, with 'victory' drawn on his round shield sitting by his feet.

Laughing, he threw back his mane of black hair and gestured toward where the two friends sat across the cleared grove, sitting in a site identical to where he stood. Stetes had slept soundly under the stars, not at all worried about what his rival would do the next day, instead of writing and erasing glyphs in the dirt all night like his foe. Tiech could see his tusked lips moving, but he could not hear what the burly orc was saying, nor did he have to. He was just glad that Ieltsech could not as well.

He had never seen his friend like this, and he had been on at least a hundred hunting trips with him. When facing down a wild beast Ieltsech was fearless – Tiech had even watched him single-handedly take down the moose whose antlers now donned the robe of their clan's shaman. But now his eyes would not leave the dirt, and his breathing was long. It was not creating a pretty image for himself, unlike Stetes' charismatic boldness.

"Your armor is here right?" Tiech spoke up finally, just to try and break the tension. He knew perfectly well it was in the ferns behind the log, it had been there all night since his friend had come to sleep by the grove. Tiech had told him that he would leave him alone that evening, but in reality he had pitched his tent within sight of his friend to keep an eye on him. As far as he could tell, his friend had not left this position for the entire cold alpine night.

Ieltsech merely nodded, to which Tiech turned to grab the leather sack and heft it onto the ground in front of them. "Maybe we should test the fitting then," Tiech continued, opening the large sack and grabbing out an arm piece. "It's not like you wear this all that often, could use some polishing too."

"Need to get painted first," grunted the grim orc, who had just kicked the dirt in front of him to clear away the words he had written. That was probably wise, because even though his friend had not been reading closely, he couldn't help but notice that some of the stuff had been rather embarrassing.

"You do not," chuckled Tiech with as much mirth as he could muster. "Stetes practically slept in his, and they seem to have gotten him painted just fine."

"He lives in iron," mumbled Ieltsech, once again back at the dirt with the bottom of his hilt. "I fight in hide."

"That is because you fight mighty beasts of the wild with the spear and bow," his friend said as he tightened the iron plate around Ielt-sech's arm, "not piddly men who hide behind walls and gates. You don't even need a shield, just took it off the llama for the first time in years to fight this fight, didn't you? Always sitting at the back of your tent when I come to visit!"

"Stetes is no great beast," the nervous orc grunted, protesting in word, but not resisting his friend's moves to robe him in metal, "and we have to fight this fight with the axe, not the spear. When have I lifted an axe in my life other than to challenge some pines?"

"Oh that is no tree-felling axe," Tiech laughed. "That is the axe of Lrades, the slayer of Dragons! A gift from the dwarves for the defense of their valley – and, if I remember correctly, the axe with which he won your mother." He winked at the last remark, trying to encourage his friend. It actually did seem to cheer him a little, as he quietly contemplated the axe for awhile after that was said, and Tiech let him.

But finally, Ieltsech planted the hilt back in the dirt and sighed. "Perhaps, but it is not like I have killed Dragons," he said gloomily.

"Well, neither had your father," his friend reminded him. "He was always the first to tell people it was just a thrashing salamander. But still, it had killed three others who had challenged it, so it's not like it wasn't an accomplishment. Besides, I seem to remember you holding your own against another kind of beast several times before." He grabbed Ieltsech on the shoulders and shook him a bit after getting his scaled cuirass in place. This finally got him to smile, albeit a bit nervously.

"You know as well as I do that if she didn't think I was cute, we would both been dead there," he said. "Pushing that close to the Bounding Deer's swine herds was a bad idea, and if I remember right, you're the one who keeps getting us over there."

To this Tiech shrugged, "Their pigs look so much like wild boars I have trouble distinguishing the two. But I'm hunting with a clan friend, so how bad could it have been?"

"You have benefited more from my aunt having won a husband from their clan than I have," Ieltsech said shaking his head, a lop-sided grin now on his face with one tusk raised a bit over the other. However, his eyes still betrayed his worry: he had caught sight of the great hulk across the way laughing with the crowd of other warriors gathered around him.

Tiech knew his rival's confidence alone would be enough to dishearten his friend, so instead he tried to keep Ieltsech's eyes on the prize instead of the competition. "Definitely not," he said quickly as he removed his friend's hunting boots to replace them with a pair clad in iron. "I don't remember being introduced to beautiful warrior women at midsummer feasts. I'm just stuck here where everyone is my sister or my second cousin."

"Oh, you meet plenty of them out in the woods," Ieltsech finally chuckled in reply. "You seem to have a knack for conjuring them up by straying too close to other clans' encampments."

"Yes, yes, yes," his friend shook his head laughing as he inspected the helmet for notches in it. "But those situations don't tend to go quite the same way as when we bump into Lresech. Although several of them are rather gorgeous... Maybe I should follow your lead and challenge one of them for their hand."

"Ha! And then get your butt kicked," a new voice sassed from behind the two of them. Into the little campsite came a young woman holding a large bowl full of red paint haphazardly under her arm.

"How would you know, you've never seen me fight!" Tiech shot back at her, "When was the last time you saw me fight Pheprats?"

The orc girl put her giant hand to her lips and scrunched her eyebrows in feigned thought. The beaded braids emerged from her head scarf as she shook herself back and forth, replying with her whole body, "Let's see, there was the hunting disagreement between you and Cieg, the tent-pitching disagreement between you and Shelt, and the…"

"Okay, okay, you can shut up," he said as he waved away the long list of losses. "Still, I can dream."

"Just like this dreamer," she sighed as she bent down in front of Ieltsech, who once again had gone quiet. "Alright then brother, what do you want on your forehead for this fight?" The comment was met with mumbling from the combatant, which only seemed to heighten his sister's snark, "Speak up dork, or I'll be picking for you."

"Might as well," he grumbled under his breath. "I've been working on this all night, and I've got nothing." For the first time concern seemed to cross his sister's face, and she stole a glance at his friend who confirmed with a look all that had been going on that morning.

"Well, then no complaining when I pick something stupid," she snorted at Ieltsech, placing the bowl on the ground between his feet. Dipping her fingers into the thick liquid that smelled like wild berries, they came out the same color as her beads and the patterns on her shawl. It was a cheap dye, but looked good enough none-the-less for someone of a hunter rank. "I don't got much time though, so Sech will have to deal with whatever I come up with on the fly."

"Maybe if someone hadn't overslept, she would have more time to think about it," Tiech chuckled from the sideline, to which he drew a glare from Pheprats as she pondered what to paint on her brother's face.

"I rested up well and fully because I knew my brother wouldn't," she said, sticking out her tongue at Tiech. "And it's not like you've done anything but sit here awkwardly all morning anyway."

"Hey," the orc hunter replied defensively, "who do you think got him in all this? I've been working hard all morning." He tugged a bit on Ieltsech's iron plates to prove his productivity.

"Okay fine, you win," she said, rolling her eyes. "And by the way brother, I just had an

idea strike me with the same amount of rash-
ness as your choice to challenge that creature
over there, and you're stuck with it now."
As she got to work with her fingers on her
brother's forehead, one hand drenched in dye
and the other holding back the ridge of hair
along the top of Ieltsech's scalp. Tiech, mean-
while, sat waiting and looking warily towards
the monstrous rival at the other side.

Still showing no sign of uneasiness, Stetes
was eating an early lunch of quail and cheese
before the ritual combat would ensue at noon.
So far, he'd had the courtesy to not try and directly mock Ieltsech across the spruce-shroud-
ed grove, but his mere muscular presence and
reputation were enough on their own. Tiech
had to wonder again at his friend's madness
in choosing this course. He likely walked toward his own death – or at least crippling
– against that viscous opponent, although
maybe Stetes' skill would be so much greater
than Ieltsech's that he would be able to take
out his rival without seriously harming the

hunter. Winning was not really a possibility here, in Tiech's eyes, and if it were for anyone but Lresech, he likely would have told Ieltsech how stupid he was being.

But instead, another word came to his mind, and so he grabbed his friend's round shield and nudged Pheprats, who was also hard at work, "If you don't mind I think I'll do the shield, just had a great idea for it."

"Go for it," she grunted, not moving from her position (which Tiech realized was blocking Ieltsech's opponent from sight), "just don't embarrass me with your art skills, 'cause they're all going to think I did it."

"No promises," Tiech retorted, moving the paint bowl and starting quickly before she could change her mind. The time passed in silence as Pheprats methodically drew each line with great detail and Tiech quickly brushed paint onto the shield's surface with his hands to catch up with her progress. With only a few minutes to spare, they finally put down the paint bowl to look at their masterpieces.

With red hands and smeared faces, they stood back from Ieltsech, who donned his shield and helm, trying to strike as fierce a pose as he could. He was hoping to get some remarks on how impressive he looked, but instead his sister screamed seeing his shield and head at the same time.

Taking Tiech by the scruff of his woolen shirt, she lifted him off the ground and shook the poor soul. "What were you thinking!" she growled at him. "We can't send him out there like that!" Immediately Ieltsech's face lost any form of fierceness he had mustered and fell back into despair.

"It's not my fault we had the same idea," the hunter shouted back, unhanding himself from Pheprats' grip, but the red smears from where she had grabbed him remained as a reminder of their mistake. "If you had been working faster I might have been able to see what glyph you were writing before I got started on my own."

"Yes, but now he looks pathetic!" she growled, yanking on her black braids as she turned back to her brother, the beads rattling as she shook her fists in frustration. "Charging into battle with 'brave' written on his face and shield just screams 'I'm terrified and going to lose!'"

"I thought 'brave' was rather fitting, considering the circumstances," muttered Tiech defensively, his eyes unable to meet Ieltsech's from under his heavy-set brow. Now Ieltsech was sweating profusely, and he could feel his legs giving out from under him. He had known this was a risky idea from the moment he first rashly challenged the hulking beast across the way, but this mess-up sealed his fate. He had been relying on at least impressing Lresech with this display, but now even that seemed out of the question.

"Oh no, she'll be coming into the grove any minute now," Pheprats grimaced as she looked up at the sun, almost reaching its zenith. "We don't have time to fix it... Just tuck your helmet down farther and maybe no one will notice."

"I could go grab my shield," Tiech offered quickly, "as a mark-less shield would probably be better than a double 'brave'." But he was too late in his offer. From the top end of the grove a horn sounded, and out from the trees walked Lresech, starting the competition to earn her hand. Ieltsech could not hesitate at this point without totally forfeiting his dignity, and thus he took in a deep breath and charged forward into the clearing, while his friends watched nervously from the sideline.

The feet of the two iron-clad competitors kicked up the dust, the metal plates sewn into their thick leather padding glinted in the sunlight unobscured by tree or cloud. The great light and the mountains towering around them would be their witnesses when their solid square axes clashed against each other's shield. It was all as customed: the glade had been cleared of all brush, an easy task since it was used often by the clans as they moved in and out of the area for such ritual fights, so often in fact that the great shaman poles had never been taken down. The very poles which would make this combat binding.

Six of them stood in a hexagon around the arena, carved with the orcish glyphs calling on the will of Death to guide this fight, although it was not common for combatants to die in such rituals. This was not a raid or a war, this was a dispute, and thus the laws of the challenge would be observed, with the bride as the witness to these events. However, the combatants were usually far more evenly matched. Underdogs usually were wise enough not to challenge an opponent as great as Stetes, but few were also as motivated as this one.

As the two met in the middle, standing there looking cautiously at each other, Ieltsech could not help but glance at Lresech. She was at the edge of the grove, standing just within the ring to judge the dispute. The glance was only brief, as to gaze longingly could be perceived as weakness, but he merely wanted to see her face one last time before he died trying to earn it. She had done extra for the occasion, her hair filled with blue beads and fitted with golden rings that in turn also sported those same blue ornaments, the color of her clan. They looked heavy to him, but he knew her neck held strong even if it was hidden underneath her deer-hide scarf. She was a warrior, and was built hardy enough to carry however much ornamentation she desired. It was actually rather strange to see her without her armor on, almost as strange as it would have been to see Stetes without his.

Like everything about him, Stetes' shield and axe were also large, seemingly as large as the crowd gathered by his end of the arena. Among humans or elves, Ieltsech would have been perceived as tall, but his rival would have been a giant. Out from under the shadow of his segmented helmet came the monster's two large tusks and the steam of his breath in the cool alpine air, the sun only just beginning to burn away the morning chill. He looked to the friends watching in horror like some gigantic demon more than an orc, like he was channeling the spirit of some god. Fortunately the fighters were in the same clan, and thus Tiech doubted he would have much success trying to get their clan god to pick favorites, although if said god had one it would probably be Stetes.

It did not help that Stetes had also come from a long line of warriors, and Tiech could feel their spirits watching from the other side of the field. Not one of them had died away from the battlefield, a boast that the gigantic warrior would also probably be able to make by the end. Ieltsech had a noble line as well, skilled hunters and pastoralists each of them, but there was not as much glamour in that. Only the Dragon Slayer really had a name for himself, and other than obtaining the antlers which donned the head of the very shaman observing this rite, Ieltsech had nothing to go by.

They stood there for a few seconds only, but it seemed like an eternity before Stetes finally raised his axe and shield to the air and called out in a deep rumbling voice, "Well-met, hunter, I would have thought you'd have better prey than me today?" Tiech had been hoping they would skip the bantering and go straight to the fighting, but he should have known the warrior wouldn't miss a chance to mock his opponent.

"I do," Ieltsech replied in a rather formal way. It was clear that it was Lresech he was meaning, the one he was really trying to prove himself to. There was just a boulder in his way to doing so. Sadly, the boulder was more of a mountain, and had an attitude to match.

"What a brave statement to make as the underdog here," chuckled the gigantic orc. "Or doubly brave, should I say. Needed the mark twice, once for each word you would dare utter against me." From behind him came the ringing laughter of the gathered crowd. Naturally the entirety of both clans were there to witness this event, spread out between the trees and conical tents to watch the fight that would ensue. Everyone had taken the time off from their work, excepting the children who could be found making sure the pigs and goats did not escape into the woods while no one was looking. Even the dogs, it seemed, showed up to watch the show, large elkhounds and bear dogs laying at their master's feet. Barking their thunderous barks as their owners jeered at the unfortunate circumstances concerning Ieltsech's war paint.

To all this the hunter made no remark – there was no point in it, and it would probably look braver to say nothing than something foolish. Although Tiech noted it did play into Stetes' accusations, which made him uncomfortable for his friends position, but there was nothing he could do. The fight had already begun with words; soon blows would follow. From beside him, though, he could hear Pheprats muttering to their father, asking for his strength to guide her brother's arm. A short and formulaic prayer, and without any burnt offerings, probably not effective, but their old man had always struck Tiech as the generous sort. Maybe the Dragon Slayer would guide that axe once again anyway. It was worth a try at least – Ieltsech would need all the help he could get.

Perhaps Lrades was communing with the spirit of Lresech's late father right now as well, a sudden thought that comforted the worried friend. They had been battle brothers in life, and that is how Ieltsech had met his precious Sech in the first place. Perhaps in death they would finish what they had started in life. Tiech decided to give his mother a try too, taking some crushed pine-cone dust from a pocket and sprinkling it free into the breeze. She had always been fond of his hunting partner, and might be willing to lend aid to him, as well with her hunting prowess. Never had he seen anyone as good with a spear and the hunting dogs, or the belt for that matter.

No prayers seemed to be offered from the other side, though, probably because they didn't think they would be necessary. The only dust or smoke in the wind over there were from pipes or the shaman's brazier, as he said a few words to the past clan elder, then the god of the clan, and then to Death himself, asking for him to show his judgment in the fight to come. After the formalities were done, he stepped back out of the area and nodded to the young woman standing beside him. Tiech couldn't help but notice that he looked a little sad – after all, this was the hunter who had gotten him such fine antlers and the moose-skin robe that proved the tribe's might. It would be an unfortunate loss if one of their great hunters were to pass away in a ritual combat, but that was the way of it.

Lresech's face had been stone cold the whole time, looking at neither of the combatants nor the priest. She was steeling herself, Tiech knew, and didn't want to accidentally reveal with her expression that she expected the worst out of this fight. She had worn that face since three days ago, when the great warrior had challenged her for her hand, and unexpectedly the hunter had risen to intercept it. This would be the talk of the tribe for many days to come, and there might even be a song sang about him. If he did well enough it might even be good. But whether for good or ill, Lresech did not express any emotion on the issue, intending to maintain her stoic warrior beauty until the end, which is probably why she had been so desirable in the first place.

As she lifted the horn to her lips to start the fight, Tiech couldn't help but notice this beauty. Her arms were strong like trees, and her tusks shown like silver on either side of the ram's horn as it touched her lips. How lucky his friend would have been if some upstart warrior hadn't challenged her before he did. Tiech was sure she at least would have gone easy enough on Ieltsech for him to barely sneak the victory over her. But, with the warrior in his way, he would never get that chance. Stetes would not be so kind.

Sure enough the moment the echoing call of the horn rang through the mountain-tops, the behemoth came upon his opponent with the deadly arc of his axe. Ieltsech could not stand his ground as the great weight of the warrior's blow struck him, and he barely was able to glance the axe off his shield and out of the way as he stepped to the side to avoid the incoming bulk of the huge warrior. With the 'glory' written upon his forehead already fulfilled, Stetes bashed his opponent in the face with 'victory', coming in for another cut before Ieltsech would even have the chance to recover.

Both of his companions watched their good friend nervously as he got pummeled. Tiech even thought he could hear a dog barking to bemoan his fate, but they stayed respectfully back. To interfere in the fight would bring shame on the combatants; it would be better for the hunter to simply die unaided in the arena. Off toward the right Lresech stood rigidly watching the progress. As Ieltsech took a particularly nasty blow to the shield, his arm visibly shuddered under the impact, but even then she did not wince. Nor did she smile, her tusked lips remained pursed in an unreadable stony look. The stoic warrior beauty that had gotten her into this position to begin with.

The other orcs jeered. It wasn't really good sport, as Stetes was just battering his rival across the grove, but they would take what they could get. Ieltsech was always on the defensive, starting to cringe with every sore movement he made while the clan warrior barely even sweated. His eyes showed amusement rather than fear or focus – there was no way the hunter could best him, and everyone knew it. The only person who did not display this confidence was Lresech herself; ever expressionless, one hand gripping tightly the horn, and the other dangling near her axe. Not threateningly, just limply, there was nothing it could do now.

A feint later, and the green-skinned warrior finally made his first direct blow. Skirting around the shield covered in the word 'brave', the axe came firmly into the side of Ieltsech. His bellow of pain was met by the braying of dogs, their booming voices growling in protest of their favorite hunter's beating. But the orcs cheered at the sight of the first blood as the combatant pulled away, leaving a gash in the side of his armor. If it were not for the iron plates and thick gambeson, he would have gotten a lot worse than several shattered ribs.

As Ieltsech staggered backwards, dazed with the pain, Tiech sucked in a long breath, renewing his prayer to his mother's spirit. He knew it was hopeless, but he had to try something or his friend might actually be killed in combat. His eyes were so focused on the battlefield and his mind on his prayer that he didn't even know something big was coming up behind, barking loudly all the way. If Pheprats had not turned and tackled the bear dog just in time the beast would have bolted straight into the arena. Tiech jumped at the sight, "Cialrces! I thought we tied you up last night!"

"We underestimated his strength," Pheprats grunted as she grappled with the gigantic wolf-like dog. A rope, sure enough, was wound tightly around his neck, trailing a few feet behind him to where it looked like it had been chewed apart. Tiech was not surprised at this turn of events; all it took was one look at the gray dog's broad snarl to see how it had been done. Saliva dripped from its barred thick teeth as the dog tried to break free to bound to his master's aid.

"Tiech!" Pheprats added quickly. "Did you hear me? Help me hold him down!" Reluctantly the hunter moved down to help keep the dog from getting loose. He wanted more than anything to let it go to Ieltsech's aid, but that would be as bad as interfering himself. Better to die in battle than live in shame.

It got easier to hold him, however, as the battle had slowed down. The combatant was trying to keep his stance, but it was obvious by the angle of Ieltsech's torso that the pain was overwhelming. Stetes did not hurry to take him on again, but stood there smiling, knowing he had already won. Cialrces' pointed ears faced directly at the huge orc, and he growled fearlessly at the gigantic beast of a man. He was trained to hunt moose and mountain mastodons – a puny orc did not scare him, but it sure did frighten those holding him down.

Finally, the opponent spoke, "That looks painful, and you have not even landed a blow on me, good hunter. Perhaps we should call it here, you leave with your life and honor intact, proving you surely are as brave as you boast, and I with my worth proven." It seemed so quick, but then again there was a skill gap there. A good orc would know when to retreat, there was no shame in that, but this wasn't about loot or other meager things. To Ieltsech, this was much more than a dispute, and at that he set his jaw flat and stood as straight as he could. The grim look in his eyes told Stetes everything he needed to know about whether he'd be surrendering or not.

With pity in his eyes, but an amused smile, the opponent merely shrugged his shoulders, "I forgot, you have two bravery marks to prove. Your spirit will be blessed for this, although it is too bad you never left it heirs for that blessing to pass to." Then, without another word, he charged across the glade. His footsteps were like thunder, his body like the wild auroch and Ieltsech's like a frail tree. The hunter took the body slam head on, the shield bearing 'victory' smashing across his face. Tiech could not look, and as he heard the sound of his friend's body hit the ground, he closed his eyes. Taking the chance of the hunter loosening his grip, Cialrces pulled himself free and bolted at the giant.

Stetes was not expecting interference from the audience, and paid no heed to the large canine barreling his way. His eyes were locked on Ieltsech. No longer did they smile, for even as much as Stetes enjoyed combat, taking a clansman's life was not a pleasant event. Still, he had not surrendered, so there was little choice left, and as the combatant lay on the ground roaring with pain, the warrior's axe hand raised above his head. In that deadly arc, no helm would save Ieltsech's life. That would have been it, if the bear dog hadn't leaped into the air, his bone-crushing jaws opened wide. Too late did the warrior spot his new opponent, and his eyes widened as the huge teeth sank into his sword arm. Now was his turn to let out a cry of fury as the huge animal pulled the orc to the dust as well. If Tiech and Pheprats had not been running to stop the beast, it would have gone for the throat next.

Their eyes were wide as they looked at the shaman standing off to the side. This was a serious offense, not only to the warrior and their friend but to Death himself in his sacred arena. At the very least the dog would have to die, if not them too. Already the angry mob around the glade was shouting curses at them, ready to stone the two trespassers themselves, but the shaman's eyes were only filled with sadness.

"Enough," he called, quieting the crowd a bit. "I think Death has spoken well enough just now. Ieltsech, you have proven your bravery twice, and I believe the dog was sent to save your life. I declare you incapacitated and thus defeated. Stetes has proven his worth!"

As the crowd cheered the shaman tried not to show partiality by clapping with them, but his pained smile showed his real opinions on the issue. He really did like his robe, after all, antlers and all. This was the most he could repay.

The victor managed a grimacing grin as he worked his way painfully to his feet. His satisfaction was only broken to throw a dirty look at the dog who had mangled his hand before he started marching down the grove to where the bride was waiting. As he did, so did she begin to move. She came slowly, the stony look she had on her face the entire fight still resting there. She did not look at the warrior, but instead stopped near the body of the fallen combatant, breathing in huge gasps on the ground. At first Tiech thought she was coming over to Ieltsech, hoping she somehow saw something the rest of them didn't, but she had not. She stopped short, looking down at something on the ground, as the victor strutted straight up to the lady in waiting.

"Well," Stetes attempted to say softly, "it has been decided." A tusked grin managed to make it past the pain in his hand as he winked, "Come, my lady, my tent awaits once I get this hand fixed up." But she did not move. Instead, she knelt down and picked something out of the dust. A look of confusion replaced the one of satisfaction when Lresech arose from the dirt carrying an axe in her hand, the one who had been dropped from the hand of the defeated. The axe of the Dragon Slayer sat loosely in her palm, and seeing this threw the entire crowd off guard.

Into the silence that followed came the gruff voice of Stetes, who was clearly not impressed by this move, "It is sad that such a prestigious weapon has failed. But that just confirms where Death stands, I suppose. There is no use, my wife, it had its chance and now it will forever be tainted with failure." But he did not seem so confident when Lresech lifted her eyebrow at the huge warrior. She might have been a whole head shorter than the giant, but Tiech swore he saw him flinch when she glared directly into his eyes.

"Your wife?" she said coldly, pausing to let her will be heard throughout the crowd. "I don't remember you ever proving your worth to me." Then she grinned, and the blood now could be seen draining from the wounded warrior's face. From her side she drew the axe of her own father, and with one in each hand she began to approach the goliath of an orc, "Or are you not brave enough to finish the ritual? Come, Death has given you the right to challenge the bride, now come and face me!"

Tiech heard a quiet chuckle from beside him as Pheprats loosened her grip on Cialrces a bit. If he had not latched onto the dog tighter, it would have charged, but instead it let out a snarl that managed to get a jump out of the great warrior, who turned to his side to try and keep both the dog and his new challenger in sight. "Lresech! I proved my worth, even with interference! With my hand as such do we really need to carry on?" he shouted more at the shaman than at his opponent, but if he thought he was going to get the support of their spiritual leader, he was mistaken.

"You have only proven you are worthy to fight her, thus far," he said with a shrug. "If she feels that was not enough to prove your strength, she has the right to have satisfaction in combat. After all, this arena has been prepared to hold duels to prove your worth to the good warrior. If you are strong enough to claim her, prove it now." Exasperated, looking from his hand to the shaman, Stetes looked like he was about to protest, and Tiech had to admit making him fight with a bad hand was a little unorthodox. Granted, challenges between two orcs over someone else were fairly rare when chieftains weren't involved. Usually it was the groom overcoming the bride or the other way around, so he wasn't going to pretend he knew the code of conduct here. The crowd seemed to have a similar sentiment, as they held their breath while Lresech began her charge, and the mighty warrior barely had his shield in place by the time her first strike was coming down on his head.

The hush that followed was well warranted, for even Tiech, who had watched this warrior woman fight many times, was amazed with what he saw. It was almost like the first fight had been inverted, and now the mighty warrior was the lowly hunter on the run. He did try, but without his weapon hand he was at a severe disadvantage. If it were still Ieltsech in the combat, Stetes probably could have bested him with just his shield, but Lresech was no hunter, she was a warrior herself, and she was on the offensive. The axe of Lrades and her father both whirled around her, and the blue beads in her hair splayed outwards and caught the sunlight as she swung. Her strikes were so hard her black locks began to escape from her tight headdress, and her arms moved with such synced skill it was almost as if they had a life of their own. For a moment Tiech wondered if they had.

It seemed like there were two warriors fighting and not one, and for a second he almost imagined the spirits of her father and the Dragon Slayer standing there instead of her, both with their hands at their axes and bringing them down with power upon their common foe. He would have thought himself crazy to have suspected the influence of both ancestral spirits, but the gasp from Pheprats confirmed his suspicions. Her prayer had been answered against the odds, just not in the way they had thought, and as the ballad of violence continued his suspicion only strengthened with each axe stroke.

Stetes stood no chance against Lresech herself in this state, let alone with assistance from her ancestors. Perhaps it would have gone differently if Stetes had called upon his own, but no prayers had been offered and thus no help came. It was amazing he had held on as long as he did, until finally he caught the flat of an axe straight in his chest, and hit the ground with a deep thud.

Dust covered Tiech's eyes for only a second,

but that was all the warrior woman needed to declare victory. By the time he had rubbed it from his vision, she was kneeling on her opponent's breastplate, only a span away, both axes crossed at his throat. Fire was in her eyes, but it was not angry, almost excited. In the dust Tiech felt like he could see the shadows of two men, each laying a hand proudly on her shoulder, but the next minute they were gone. As happy as he was, the thought made him roll his eyes. Of course everyone besides his stubborn mother showed up, even in death she was a pain.

Then Cialrces let out another angry bark, although he had stopped struggling so much, and Tiech suddenly remembered his thought earlier on how she had always been good with dogs. "Oh, mother," he whisper quietly, "you could have ruined everything, but thanks anyway, I do appreciate my friend being alive." In response he felt the phantom pain of her belt again, but as he rubbed his rear it was gone, and he knew that for once she was proud of him for inviting her to the fight.

Back in the realm of the living, however, a loud roar of approval had arisen from the crowd. They whooped and cheered even louder at Lresech's victory than they had at Stetes'. She had given them quite the show and demonstrated battle prowess that could have beaten him even with his hands in use – they were satisfied. The shaman especially wore a rather smug look on his face. "Well then, Lresech," his deep voice chuckled as he actually clapped this time, "I suppose no one will ever assume you're impressed again, young men will think twice before challenging you."

"They need not," she said, her axes still at her opponent's throat, "for I will lay claim soon enough that they won't have the chance." It took Stetes laying on the ground a few seconds to catch on to what she had said, but when he did his eyebrows furrowed in anger, and his raspy breathing got louder.

"You dare!" his voice carried over the cheering and might have even echoed off the mountains he was so angry. "He was beaten fairly, he could not back up his own challenge! You would dare to take a weakling who could not prove his own strength? You could have had someone who had proven his own worth! Why choose dishonor? Why Lresech?" His growl was surprisingly sharp for someone with twin axe blades at their throat, but then again Tiech supposed he was probably used to that. He was a warrior after all, and Tiech had to begrudgingly admit he was very good at his job.

Stetes' words were great insults to her dignity – cherishing weakness was not taken lightly amongst the orcs anywhere on the earth – but she did not seem phased by his accusations. Instead she replied calmly, and Tiech watched her gaze shift from her opponent as she spoke. "I want the one who faced certain death to have me," she said boldly. "Only the strongest can face down the lion when they know it will kill them. Any coward can fight those weaker than them, and I don't think we can call Ieltsech a coward. He earned both marks of bravery before he even stepped into this glade."

Then, without another word she planted her father's axe in the ground just above Stetes' neck, signaling his defeat whether he would like to surrender or not. If he so much as moved he would slit his own throat, and removing the axe with his bad hand would take time, but it didn't matter. He was in too much pain to keep fighting anyway, so she turned her back confidently on him and toward the other warrior laying in the dirt.

Ieltsech simply lay there in the dirt, waiting. His hand was now clutching his side, and his breaths were still long and sharp, but the pain seemed to be under control now. With calm eyes he watched the beautiful warrior woman approach, and they never left her face even as she lowered his own axe between them. The blade touched the ridge of his nose, but he just kept staring up into her eyes, and Tiech could not imagine the amount of bliss he had to be in right now. From beside him he heard a quiet retching noise, and turned to see Pheprats grabbing her stomach in mock illness, but her grin betrayed how happy she was to see this turn of events.

"Ieltsech of the Howling Gale clan," she said loudly, for all to hear, "I challenge you for your hand. Prove your worth and you may keep it, otherwise I will claim it in the spoils of victory. May Death see the right party victorious."

To this he closed his eyes, and grabbed the back of the axe and moved it from his face to his throat. The axe his father had won his mother over with now had defeated him, and Tiech couldn't help but laugh inside about how sickening the sappiness of it all was. Pheprats' response had been the correct one, but he was happy for his friend none-the-less. "Then I surrender my hand," Ieltsech said as steadily as he could, a smile attempting to break through the pain of his broken ribs, "for I know I cannot best you in battle even if I was not wounded on the ground."

That was that. The shaman happily clapped his hands and declared the combat binding. Without anymore hesitation, the orc warrior scooped up her husband from the ground and carried him off the battlefield. It would take weeks for those ribs to heal, but that did not seem to quiet the flames of victory in her eyes – she was so eager to get started that she left both of her weapons behind in the arena. Hesitantly the two onlookers let go of the big dog as the crowd's cheers became so loud Tiech thought the men hiding behind their walls miles away were probably cowering in terror. Little did they know that this was actually a happy event and not the harbinger their doom. Cialrces wagged his tail happily having been released from his bondage, and after being given a stick so he wouldn't chomp down on someone else's arm he bounded away after the happy couple, excited to be at his master's side once again.

As Pheprats went to go pick up her father's axe from the dirt, Tiech felt a tap on his shoulder. Turning, he came face to face with Stetes, carrying the axe that had beaten him in combat. At first Tiech almost let out a yelp as he looked far up into the face of the gigantic warrior, who he figured was still angry about his defeat, but he needn't have worried. The axe's handle, not the blade, was facing him, and as their eyes met, a mutual nod of respect was made. Tiech took the axe without comment. Then the big warrior turned around and walked back to his friends who, although visibly shocked, began to work on mending his mangled hand.

Against all the odds he had lost, but that is the way of it. There was no shame in losing to a warrior of Lresech's skill, it was just not expected from a hulking fighter such as himself. For a few moments Tiech looked down at the axe he had been given and wondered to himself whether he might be able to beat the odds as well. Perhaps Death would be lenient and let him beat one of those pretty warrior women he kept "bumping into" out hunting with Ieltsech.

But before the question got too ingrained in his head, a voice broke his thoughts from across the glade. "Come on, doofus," Pheprats shouted at him as she waved the other axe in her hand. "We got to go sharpen that hunk of metal you're holding before she notices how much she blunted it by stabbing it in the ground... and then probably polish it since you have your dirty mitts all over it." Tiech nodded in response with a sly grin creeping over his face. On second thought, maybe there was some sassy orc he needed to prove he could win a battle to, and with that thought in mind he followed off happily after her. They had blades to sharpen after all.

Appendix

Ieltsech: (Orcish: *Íeltssech* /jəlts'əx/)

One of the two contestants fighting for the right to challenge Lresech for her hand. A gifted hunter, but not a particularly gifted warrior.

Tiech: (Orcish: *Tíech* /tʲəx/)

Ieltsech's best friend and hunting partner, as well as his main support during the ritual combat.

Pheprats: (Orcish: *Phefprats* /pˠəvpra͡ts/)

Ieltsech's sister, who also comes to support him at the ritual combat.

Lresech: (Orcish: *Lrésech* /lresəx/)

The subject of the ritual combat and childhood friend of Ieltsech. Considered a very beautiful and skilled warrior, which has lead to the event of there being multiple suitors fighting for the right to challenge her for her hand in marriage.

Cialrces: (Orcish: *Cíalrcés* /kʲalrkˈes/)

A large Bear Dog that belongs to Ieltsech's hunting pack. He is very loyal to his owner to the point of needing to be tied up during the ritual combat.

Stetes: (Orcish: *Stsétés* /st͡setes/)

The opponent fighting Ieltsech for the right to challenge Lresech for her hand. A confident and well seasoned warrior, renowned for his skills by the clan.

Lrades: (Orcish: *Lradés* /lrades/)

Ieltsech's late father who was also a skilled hunter and friend of Lresech's father. He had been given the name of "Dragon Slayer" for killing a Thrashing Salamander many years back.

Cieg: (Orcish: *Cíeg* /kʲeg/)

A fellow orc in the clan who Tiech lost a hunting dispute to in ritual combat.

Shelt: (Orcish: *Shélt* /s'elt/)

A fellow orc in the clan who Tiech lost a tent pitching dispute to in ritual combat.

About the Author...

At the age of six years old, living in Whatcom County in Washington State, just shy of the Canadian border, Gabriel Huffman was sat down by his father and read "The Hobbit" by J.R.R. Tolkien. That small event kick-started his lifelong interest in writing fantasy and how the genre could be used beyond its typical bounds. Twenty years and a computer science degree from Western Washington University later, he had all the tools and willpower necessary to finally publish his first short story: "To Face a Lion". Though writing is his main form of art, he truly just loves being immersed in the joy and wonder of making things and hopes he was able to share a little bit of that joy with you.

9 781963 222036